Gabriella
the Snow Kingdom Fairy

For Alex Goodfellow, with lots of love.

Special thanks to
Sue Mongredien

ORCHARD BOOKS
338 Euston Road, London NW1 3BH
Orchard Books Australia
Level 17/207 Kent Street, Sydney, NSW 2000
A Paperback Original

First published in 2008 by Orchard Books

HIT entertainment

Illustrations © Orchard Books 2008

A CIP catalogue record for this book is available
from the British Library.

ISBN 978 1 40830 034 3

1 3 5 7 9 10 8 6 4 2

Printed and bound in China by Imago

Orchard Books is a division of Hachette Children's Books,
an Hachette Livre UK company

www.hachettelivre.co.uk

Gabriella
the Snow Kingdom
Fairy

by Daisy Meadows

ORCHARD

It's icy cold and freezing, now that winter's here.
Snowstorms and icy sleet – my favourite time of year.
But what's this – smiling faces? People having fun?
I think I'll spoil the snow for everyone!

The Magic Snowflake I shall steal,
the Silver Chest and Firestone too.
How they'll shiver, how they'll sigh
when my work is through!

Gabriella's Magic
Snowflake

Contents

A Fairy Snowball!

"We're going to try out the snow," Kirsty Tate called to her mum. "We'll be back for lunch, OK?"

"See you later!" Rachel Walker shouted to her mum and dad.

The two friends grinned at each other as their parents called back goodbyes. Both girls were wearing new salopettes, puffa jackets, woolly hats and gloves.

Kirsty pushed open the door of the chalet, and out they stepped, blinking in the bright sunshine.

Mountain peaks rose majestically all around, covered in thick white snow. Skiers were already whizzing down the slopes, zig-zagging across the mountainside in colourful groups. Other people were careering about on snowboards, sun glinting off their snow goggles.

Rachel couldn't stop smiling. "It's so fantastic being on holiday with you again!" she said happily.

Kirsty nodded. "I know," she said, linking arms with her best friend. "All this snow, and the Winter Festival in a few days to look forward to, as well." She beamed. "And you never know, we might meet a fairy, too. We always have such magical adventures when we're together!"

The girls' parents had rented them
skis and a snowboard each, and Rachel
and Kirsty went to find them in the
small shed at the side of the chalet.
"I'm going to try my skis first," Kirsty
decided, taking a pair of ski poles, skis
and special ski boots. She sat down to
put them on, feeling tingly with
excitement.

"I'll try a snowboard," Rachel said eagerly, picking up a turquoise board that was long and slender, with rounded ends.

Once they were both ready, they found a small slope to practise on.

"Wheeee!" Kirsty squealed, pushing off. "Here I go!" She whizzed down the slope, but wobbled at the end and fell sideways into the snow. Ouch! It was hard and icy. She got to her feet gingerly, rubbing her legs.

"My turn now... Wheeee!" cried Rachel, standing on her board and riding downhill on it. It was hard keeping her balance, though, and she fell off too. "Ow!" she cried, as her elbow bumped on a particularly hard patch of ice. "This snow isn't very soft, is it?"

Kirsty shook her head. "Look at that girl over there," she murmured, helping her friend up. "The snow's so hard, she can't even build her snowman!"

Rachel watched the girl, who was struggling with her snowman nearby. The snow wasn't clumping together properly, and crumbled to ice chips instead.

"Maybe we should leave skiing and snowboarding for a bit later," Rachel suggested. "How about a snowball fight?"

"You're on," Kirsty laughed, quickly unstrapping her skis.

The girls started making
snowballs but the snow
didn't stick together
very well. And
then, when they
started throwing
them at one
another, the
snowballs were
so hard, they
really hurt!

Rachel had
just opened
her mouth to
suggest they try
something else
when she saw a
snowball zooming
towards her face. Before

she could duck, the
snowball suddenly
burst apart in a puff
of sparkling snow
crystals. Rachel
jumped in
surprise...and
then stared
as she noticed
a little fairy
hovering in
midair, right
where the
snowball had
been.

"Oh!" gasped
Rachel in surprise.
"Hello! Who are
you?"

The fairy had chestnut-brown hair with a fringe, and wore fluffy white earmuffs tipped with silver glitter. She was dressed in a purple coat with a red-and-purple striped dress underneath, red leggings and purple snow boots.

"I'm Gabriella," the fairy said, dropping a dainty curtsey. "Gabriella the Snow Kingdom Fairy. And I'm really glad to see you here!"

Kirsty came over excitedly. "Hi, Gabriella," she said to the tiny fairy. "I'm Kirsty. Is everything all right?"

Gabriella shook her head sadly. "No," she said. "Jack Frost is up to his tricks again! He's stolen my special

Magic Snowflake, which makes all the snow soft, fluffy and white. Without it, the snow everywhere is much harder and icier."

"We noticed," Kirsty said. "How did he get your snowflake?"

"Well, every year on the first of December, I hang my Magic Snowflake on the Christmas Tree outside the Fairyland palace," Gabriella explained. "But this morning the snowflake was gone — and there were goblin footprints all around the tree. I'm sure Jack Frost ordered his goblins to steal it, and hide it in the human world."

"We'll help you look for it," Rachel said at once.

"Thank you," Gabriella said gratefully. "It'll be difficult to spot, I'm afraid. The only clue will be if we see any snow that looks perfectly sparkly and fluffy. That could mean my Magic Snowflake is nearby."

Kirsty gazed around...then frowned as she noticed that it was snowing over a nearby pine forest. "How weird," she commented. "It's snowing there – but not here!" Gabriella swung round to see, her head tilted as she looked carefully at the falling flakes.

Then a smile appeared on her face. "They look like proper snowflakes to me," she declared.

"Does that mean…?" Rachel began excitedly.

Gabriella nodded. "Yes," she said. "I'm sure my Magic Snowflake must be in that forest. Let's go and look!"

Freeze!

The three friends set off to investigate. They made their way through the pine trees and saw a small clearing ahead. They could hear voices ringing out in the crisp morning air, and as they drew nearer the clearing, they saw that it was full of goblins!

"Hide!" Kirsty said, darting behind a spiky green pine tree. Rachel and Gabriella followed. They couldn't let the goblins spot them – they would guess that the girls and Gabriella were looking for the Magic Snowflake.

Rachel, Kirsty and Gabriella peeped cautiously through the branches of the pine tree. The goblins were having a great time playing in the snow…and what fluffy snow it seemed to be, too!

"My snowflake *must* be nearby," Gabriella whispered. "That snow looks perfect. And the falling flakes look so fluffy and soft, too!"

"We'll have to get closer so we can have a better look for your snowflake," Rachel hissed. "But it'll be tricky with all those goblins."

"Don't forget, guys, to keep an eye out for interfering fairies," one of the goblins said loudly just then. "Jack Frost gave me strict instructions not to let any of them near our snowflake!"

Gabriella bristled in indignation. "*Our* snowflake indeed!" she said crossly. "What a cheek!"

"Maybe if we had some kind of disguise we could creep closer," Kirsty thought aloud. "It would have to be something white, of course, with all this snow…"

Rachel grinned. "We could be snowmen!" she said. "Gabriella, would you be able to magic us to look like snowmen?"

Gabriella smiled. "Yes, of course – what a great idea," she said. "Although snowmen don't usually *walk*, do they? My magic will only make you look like snowmen while you're very still."

"OK," Kirsty said. "We'll just have to inch forwards a tiny bit at a time." She propped her skis and Rachel's snowboard by a tree. "And we'll freeze whenever a goblin looks our way."

"Talking of freezing…" Gabriella said, and waved her wand. A swirl of blue and red fairy dust shaped like tiny snowballs streamed around the girls and they immediately looked like round white snowmen, with hats and scarves and carrot noses.

"Fantastic!" Rachel chuckled, clapping her hands together. But as she moved, her own arms became visible and the snowman illusion vanished. It was only when she was perfectly still again that her disguise returned.

"This is going to be difficult," she said. "But we have to try."

"Good luck!" Gabriella whispered. The girls slowly crept nearer the goblins, stopping every time they thought one of them was going to look their way. It was very nerve-racking. Kirsty's heart thumped as she and Rachel shuffled closer and closer. They were almost near enough to hear the goblins muttering to one another. Only a few more steps and they'd be able to listen in on everything!

But just then, one of the goblins swung round and saw them. "Hey!" he shouted to his friends. "Look over there!"

A Special Discovery

Oh, no! Rachel and Kirsty could hardly breathe with fright. Had the goblin seen their human shapes? Had they been found out?

"Look at those snowmen!" the goblin said to his friends. "Cool!"

A pointy-nosed goblin stared. "Who built them?" he wondered. "I didn't notice them before." He got up as if he were about to take a closer look, and Rachel and Kirsty were both filled with dread. Oh, help! If he came too close, he'd be sure to realise they weren't *real* snowmen!

Luckily, a goblin with big ears pulled the pointy-nosed goblin back down to where he'd been sitting on a log.

"There's no time to mess about," he said sternly. "We've got to start getting ready for Jack Frost's party."

Kirsty and Rachel held their breath
as they listened in to the goblins'
conversation. It soon became clear that
Jack Frost was having a big winter
party at his Ice Castle in Fairyland. He
wanted the snow around his castle to
be perfect so everyone would have fun
playing in it — and that
was why he'd stolen
the Magic Snowflake.
"Of course, he's
even happier now
he's realised that
the rest of the
snow has been
ruined for the
fairies and the
humans!" chortled
the big-eared goblin.

Gabriella, meanwhile, had fluttered to hide behind Kirsty so that she too could listen in to the goblins. Kirsty could feel Gabriella's wings quiver crossly as she heard what the goblins were saying.

Then Rachel spotted something. Two goblins were throwing something white and sparkly to one another like a Frisbee. "Gabriella!" she hissed. "Is that your snowflake?"

Gabriella peeped over Kirsty's snowman hat. "Yes!" she squeaked. "There it is!"

The snowflake was certainly very magical. Whenever one of the goblins missed a catch and the snowflake landed on the ground, it created a huge puff of sparkling white snow all around it, like a miniature snowdrift. The goblins had to dig it out of the snow each time it happened.

Just as the girls were wondering how they would be able to get the snowflake back, the goblin nearest them missed his catch again, and the snowflake landed not far from the girls. On impulse, both

Kirsty and Rachel dashed towards it, meaning to dig the snowflake out of its snowdrift. But of course, the snowman illusion vanished – and the girls were suddenly very visible to the goblins...

Race Down the Mountain

"Hey!" cried a goblin. "Those snowmen just turned into girls!"

Kirsty and Rachel scrabbled frantically in the snow. Where was that snowflake?

"They're trying to steal our Magic Snowflake!" another goblin realised. "Quick!"

Immediately, the goblins all rushed to the snowdrift and began scooping away the snow at great speed, desperate to get to the snowflake before the girls could.

Rachel and Kirsty dug away just as urgently, but snow was now flying everywhere as the goblins shovelled and burrowed, and it was hard to see. And then…

"Got it!" cried a goblin triumphantly,

leaping to his feet with
the white sparkly
Magic Snowflake
in his hand.

"Run!" another
goblin bellowed.
He kicked a
pile of snow
into the girls'
faces, and
then he and
the other
goblins ran
to grab their
sledges and
snowboards.
Within seconds,
they were all speeding
away into the distance.

Kirsty and Rachel wiped the snow from their eyes. "Let's grab our skis and snowboard. We can't let them escape!" Kirsty cried.

"Let me help," Gabriella said, and waved her wand. Fairy dust spiralled from its tip, and the snowboard and skis rose up from where the girls had left them propped against the tree – and zoomed through the air, in a cloud of glittering blue sparkles. The snowboard landed neatly at Rachel's feet and the skis arranged themselves in front of Kirsty, with the poles flying into her hands.

The girls' snowmen disguises vanished for good.

"Thanks, Gabriella," Kirsty said, as she fastened her skis. "Let's go!"

The goblins were in the distance by now, so the girls and Gabriella gave chase. Fresh snow was falling in the wake of the Magic Snowflake, blurring their view, but the goblins were whooping and yelling and making so much noise, they were easy to track.

The goblins disappeared over the side of a mountain slope, and when Kirsty, Rachel and Gabriella reached the edge, they saw that the goblins were skimming down at top speed.

Rachel held her breath as she and Kirsty began whizzing down the slope. She hadn't had much practice on a snowboard, and this was a steep mountain – she really hoped she'd be able to keep her balance. Kirsty, too,

felt nervous on her skis. She'd only
ever tried them out on the nursery
slopes before. But both girls knew
Gabriella's fairy magic would help
them to keep up with the goblins –
it was their only hope of getting the
Magic Snowflake back!

"You're doing really well," Gabriella
called out encouragingly. "I think we're
gaining on them. Keep going!"

It was true. The girls were getting
nearer and nearer the goblins. Kirsty
could see that the goblin with the
snowflake was close to her, and she
hunched a little lower on her skis,
trying to catch up with him on his
sledge. Just as she was about to reach
him, though, another goblin whizzed
past on a snowboard, on the far side of

her – and plucked the snowflake deftly out of the first goblin's hands.

Luckily, Rachel was near the goblin who now had the snowflake. As she zoomed past on her snowboard, she flung out a hand and grabbed the snowflake from the surprised goblin.

Rachel gasped in shock – partly that she'd got Gabriella's Magic Snowflake, but also because it was so very cold to the touch, even though she was wearing gloves! It numbed her fingers, and she couldn't hold onto it properly and then…

"Oh no!" she cried helplessly, as she dropped it. Her frozen fingers just couldn't grip onto it any more. She tried desperately to stop her snowboard but she was going too fast, and could only turn and watch as the snowflake floated through the air behind her…

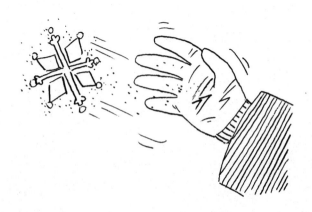

A Snowy Surprise

"Ha ha!" A goblin who was whizzing along on a sledge grabbed the Magic Snowflake and cheered with glee.

Rachel finally managed to stop her snowboard and Kirsty pulled up beside her, with Gabriella flying above.

"Sorry," Rachel groaned, feeling disappointed with herself. "I wasn't expecting it to be so cold."

"Don't worry," Kirsty said. "I've got an idea. Gabriella, do you think you could use your magic to create a huge snowdrift at the bottom of the mountain? We could catch all the goblins in it!"

"Sure," Gabriella replied. "Let's see…" She pointed her wand downwards and chanted some magical words. Blue and red sparkles crackled from her wand…and then an enormous pile of snow appeared at the foot of the mountain. The goblins, who were all careering down the slope, plunged straight into it!

52

Gabriella giggled. "It's a nice soft landing for them, at least," she said, as their muffled shouts went up. Goblin arms and legs were sticking out from the snow, but none of them seemed able to get out.

"Come on," Kirsty said with a grin. "Let's see if we can take the snowflake now all the goblins are trapped."

She and Rachel went down to the
bottom of the mountain, stopping just
before they reached the goblin snow
heap. "There it is," Rachel said
happily, seeing a green hand poking
out with its knobbly fingers
curled around the Magic
Snowflake.

"Hooray!" cried Gabriella, soaring
over. She touched the snowflake with
her wand and it immediately glowed
with bright red fairy magic, and shrank
down to its Fairyland size.

The fairy looked delighted. "Thank you, girls," she said. "Now I can put the Magic Snowflake back where it should be – on the Fairyland Christmas Tree.

And this time I'll tie it on with some magic tinsel to stop anyone trying to take it!" She kissed Kirsty and Rachel happily. "And then all the snow in Fairyland and in your world will be perfect – just what you need for winter holiday fun!"

Rachel and Kirsty beamed at the little fairy and said goodbye, then she vanished in a cloud of blue sparkles.

They turned to see that the goblins had clambered out of the snowdrift, and were stomping off, their heads down.

"That was fun," Rachel said.
"I loved whizzing down the mountain like that."

"Me too," said Kirsty. "It's turning out to be another fantastic fairy holiday...and it's only just begun!"

Contents

Stolen!

The next morning was bright and sunny. After their exciting time the day before, Kirsty and Rachel couldn't wait to get back on the slopes.

"The snow looks perfect," Rachel said happily, as she and Kirsty tramped along. "Good old Gabriella!"

"I love the way the snow creaks under our boots," Kirsty said. "It's so deep and soft — just right."

Rachel gazed around, appreciating the glittering white blanket of snow that covered everything…but then she noticed something strange. "Nobody seems very happy," she murmured to Kirsty. "I wonder why not?"

Kirsty followed her friend's gaze. Rachel was right. The other people out on the slope looked glum and bored. Nobody seemed to be in a holiday mood, or enjoying themselves even slightly.

"That's weird," Kirsty said, puzzled.
"The sun's shining, the sky's blue,
the snow's gorgeous...what's the
problem?"

"I don't know," Rachel said. "But
I've got a funny feeling something's
not right."

It started to snow just then, and the
air was full of beautiful sparkling
snowflakes flurrying in little
whirlwinds. Suddenly
Kirsty noticed one extra-
sparkly snowflake that
landed on the branch of
a nearby tree. Curious,
she went for a closer
look...and saw that
behind it was Gabriella
the Snow Kingdom Fairy!

"Rachel!" Kirsty called. "Over here!"
She hurried to see what their new fairy
friend was doing back in the human
world. What luck to see her again!

"Hello, Gabriella," Kirsty smiled.
Then her face fell as she realised that
Gabriella didn't look happy. "Is
everything all right?"

"What's the matter?"
Rachel asked, joining
Kirsty by the tree.

"It's Jack Frost again," Gabriella told
them. "This time he's stolen the magic
chest full of Festive Spirit!"

"Festive Spirit?" Kirsty echoed. "What's that?"

"It's a magic potion," Gabriella explained, "and it's kept inside a silver chest in the Fairyland palace. While it's there, it ensures that parties and special occasions are fun for all humans and fairies. And whenever there's a particularly special event, like tomorrow's festival, I release the Festive Spirit from the chest, and the celebrations become even more wonderful than expected."

Rachel remembered all the gloomy-looking people they'd seen that morning and something clicked in her mind. "Now that Jack Frost has the Festive Spirit, does that mean people won't be in a party mood?" she guessed.

"That's right," said Gabriella. "I was hoping to make the village festival really fantastic tomorrow, but if nobody feels happy, it'll be ruined!"

"How did Jack Frost manage to get hold of the potion?" Kirsty asked.

"He dressed up as a carol singer," Gabriella explained, "then sneaked into the Fairyland palace and stole the silver chest. He's taken it back to his castle."

"We'll help you

get it back," Rachel said at once.

An anxious expression crossed Gabriella's face. "That's very kind of you," she said, "but I'm afraid there's only one way we'll be able to do that." She swallowed and looked nervous. "We'll have to go into Jack Frost's castle ourselves!"

Outside the
Ice Castle

Rachel and Kirsty felt a little frightened
at the idea of going into Jack Frost's
castle. They'd been there before with
Holly the Christmas Fairy, and knew
what a cold, scary place it was.

"We've got to do it," Kirsty said after
a moment, trying to sound brave and
confident.

Rachel nodded, a determined look in her eyes. "We managed it once, so we can do it again," she agreed. "We can't let the festival be ruined!"

Gabriella smiled. "I was hoping you'd say that," she told them. "I'll take you to Fairyland right away!" She waved her wand and lots of snowball-shaped sparkles streamed around the girls.

Kirsty and Rachel felt as if they were spinning up into a whirlwind, and all they could see before their eyes were blue and red stars.

Then the mist cleared and they

were lowered to the ground again. The
three of them were standing near a
holly bush that was covered in berries.

"We're fairies!" Kirsty cheered.
She peeped over one shoulder to
examine her delicate fairy wings that
shimmered in the winter sunshine, and
couldn't resist giving
them a gentle
flutter so that she
lifted off the
ground. Oh,
how she loved
being able to fly!

Rachel fluttered
into the air too –
but as she rose up,
she saw what was
over the other side of the holly bush.

Jack Frost's Ice Castle! Rachel gulped. She'd almost forgotten why they were here, in the excitement of becoming a fairy.

The castle was built from sheets of gleaming ice, and had four towers with ice-blue turrets. Last time the girls had been here, they had thought how forbidding it looked – but today it seemed a much livelier place. Rachel

stared, then beckoned to her friends. "Have you seen what the goblins are doing?" she hissed.

Gabriella and Kirsty flew up to look. The castle was swarming with Jack Frost's goblin servants, working busily in preparation for the party.

Some goblins were hanging out icicle streamers, others were blowing up ice-blue balloons. One goblin was on the highest tower, hanging up a large flag with a picture of Jack Frost on it.

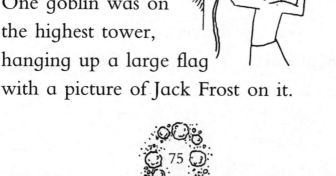

"We'll never be able to get into the castle with all those goblins around," Kirsty said in dismay.

Rachel remembered what Gabriella had said about Jack Frost managing to sneak into the Fairyland palace by posing as a carol singer. "Maybe if we disguise ourselves, we'll be able to get past the goblins," she suggested.

"How about if we're dressed as delivery people, with an urgent parcel for Jack Frost? That way they'll have to let us in!"

"Let's see if my fairy magic can make something special," Gabriella said, then waved her wand.

Glittering blue fairy dust danced in the air, and then a fabulous cake appeared, with three tiers covered in thick white frosting. A miniature slide ran all around from top to bottom, like a helter-skelter.

"Look who's on the slide!" Kirsty
cried in excitement. "A tiny model
of Jack Frost, on a marzipan sledge!"

"And here are the goblins!" Rachel laughed, pointing out the miniature green figures, throwing snowballs at each other, skiing and sledging. There were Jack Frost's beloved snow geese on a silvery icing pond. And around the side of the bottom tier read the word "Celebrate" in glittery writing.

"It's fantastic," Rachel said, smiling at Gabriella. "Amazing!"

"Thank you," Gabriella replied, blushing modestly. "Now I'd better give us all something to wear!"

She waved her wand again, and blue
sparkles tumbled around the three of
them. Kirsty and Rachel looked down
at themselves to see that they were
now wearing red delivery overalls,
which covered their wings, purple
tops and red baseball caps.

Gabriella, too, was in the delivery uniform, and quickly tucked her wand into her overall pocket.

"There," she said. "We're all ready. Let's go!"

Kirsty, Rachel and Gabriella set off for the castle with the cake. "Delivery!" they called out as they approached the huge double doors, where a pair of goblins stood guard. Icicles hung above their heads, and it was very cold.

"Special delivery for a…" Rachel pretended to be reading a label on the cake stand. "A Mr Jack Frost!"

The goblin guards were very interested in the cake when they saw it. "Ooh, cake!" said one goblin with greedy eyes. "Can we eat it now?"

"I'm starving," the second goblin said, licking his lips. He stretched out a warty finger and tried to scoop up some of the icing, but Kirsty batted him away.

"Excuse me," she said haughtily.
"I don't think Mr Frost will be very
pleased if his cake arrives with goblin
fingerprints
on it!"

The goblins
shrank back
at her words.
"Sorry," the
second goblin
muttered.

"Which way
to the kitchen,
please?" Rachel
asked briskly,
taking a step closer to the
doors. Her heart thumped and she
crossed her fingers behind her back,
willing the guards to let them in.

"Straight through the doors, take
the first corridor on your left, and
follow it round," the greedy-eyed
goblin said, pushing open the enormous
metal doors.

The girls and Gabriella stepped
inside, hardly able to believe their luck.
They had made it into Jack Frost's icy
castle! Now all they had to do was
find the silver chest containing the
Festive Spirit.

They were standing in a huge chilly
hall, with a chandelier made of ice
diamonds hanging above their heads.
"This way, I guess," Gabriella said,
pointing to where a dark, gloomy
corridor snaked away on the left.
She shivered. "Let's walk quickly, it's
freezing in here!"

The three friends made their way
down the corridor and found a large,
light kitchen at the end. A goblin chef
with a tall white hat was blending
silvery-blue ice cream when they
entered.

"We're just delivering this," Kirsty told the chef, setting the cake carefully down on a table.

The chef barely looked up from his mixing bowl. "Thanks," he said, then stared at a recipe book. "Stir until ice crystals appear," he murmured to himself.

"Um…I was just wondering," Rachel said. "I don't suppose you've seen a silver chest anywhere in the castle, have you?"

"Or a bottle of amethyst-coloured liquid?" Gabriella added hopefully.

"What's this, twenty questions?" the goblin grumbled, stirring his mixture. "I don't have time for anything except party food right now, OK?"

"So you haven't seen the silver—" Kirsty began, but the goblin looked up and glared at her.

"I'm busy!" he snapped. "Now buzz off!"

Kirsty, Rachel and Gabriella left the room quickly and huddled outside.

"What now?" Rachel wondered. "This castle is huge. The Festive Spirit could be anywhere!"

Kirsty thought hard. Then an idea floated into her head. "Would you be able to turn yourself into a really tiny fairy, Gabriella?" she said, thinking aloud. "Then you could hide in my pocket. And Rachel and I could get ourselves arrested by the guards, and—"

Rachel interrupted. "Arrested?" she echoed in shock.

"Yes," Kirsty replied. "If we're arrested, the guards are sure to take us to Jack Frost. And then we can tell him we broke in to get the Festive Spirit and…"

Rachel and Gabriella were both staring at Kirsty as if she were completely mad, but she carried on talking. "We can make Jack Frost believe that Gabriella is on her way back to Fairyland with the silver chest," she explained. "And Jack Frost is sure to panic, and rush to wherever he's keeping the Festive Spirit to see if it's still there. And then we'll find out where he's been hiding it!"

Rachel and Gabriella tried to take all of this in, both silent. "It's a clever idea," Rachel replied after a moment.

"But risky," Gabriella said, her pretty face doubtful.

"Well, I can't think of any other way to find out where the Festive Spirit is hidden, can you?" Kirsty asked them.

Her friends shook their heads.

"That settles it, then," Kirsty said. "We'll have to try. Now, how should we get ourselves arrested?"

Caught by the Guards!

"Wait," Gabriella said. "What will we do once we've found out where the Festive Spirit is? Try to grab it and fly off with it?"

Kirsty hesitated. "Um…I hadn't thought that far," she confessed. "I'm not sure. I guess we'll just have to decide on that when we come to it."

They all looked at one another. Getting taken to Jack Frost with no real escape plan seemed a very dangerous venture. But, as Kirsty said, they didn't have any other ideas right now.

"Well, here goes," Gabriella said, and sprinkled some blue and red fairy dust over herself. Immediately, she began shrinking until she was as small as Kirsty's little finger. "Will that do?" she asked, her voice a tiny squeak.

"Perfect," Kirsty said, and pulled open her pocket so that Gabriella could slip inside. Then she looked at Rachel.

"Now to get ourselves arrested!" she said, trying not to sound as nervous as she felt.

Rachel nodded. "Let's go back to the hall," she said. "We can pretend to be spying, and hope some of the goblins spot us."

Once they were in the icy hall, the two friends began prowling around, calling out to each other in loud, clear voices. "Well, she's not down here," Kirsty bellowed, pretending to search behind a tall metal cloak-stand.

"No, she's not over here either,"
Rachel shouted back, peering behind
some midnight-blue curtains at one
of the windows.

"I hope she gets away without Jack
Frost catching her!" Kirsty called.

"Oho!" came a voice just then.
"What have we here, then?"

Two goblins had appeared. Rachel
and Kirsty pretended to gasp in fright.
"Oh, no!" Rachel cried.

"We've been caught!" Kirsty wailed.

"You certainly have," one of the goblins said, stalking towards them with an unpleasant smile. "Looking for something, were you? Spying on the master's castle?"

"Take them to the dungeon!" the second goblin decided. "Let's lock 'em up. Spies deserve nothing less."

Rachel and Kirsty exchanged glances. If they were locked in the dungeon, they'd have no chance of seeing Jack Frost! "As long as you don't take us to your master," Rachel begged desperately. "He's so scary!"

The goblins looked at one another. "On second thoughts," one of them said, "let's take 'em to Jack Frost. I wonder what he'll say when we tell him you've been spying?"

"Oh no," Kirsty wailed. "We're going to be in such trouble!"

The goblins looked pleased at her words. "Yes, you are," they said, taking Kirsty and Rachel by their wrists. "This way!"

The goblins hauled the girls along a stone corridor into the Great Hall.

Jack Frost was sitting at the end of the room, on an enormous icy throne. He looked up when he saw the girls enter with his guards, and a suspicious gleam came into his eyes. "You two!" he said, recognising Kirsty and Rachel, despite their uniforms. "What are you doing here?"

"Spying, they were," one of the
goblins said, pushing the girls roughly
towards Jack Frost. "We caught 'em!"

"Spying, eh?" Jack Frost glared at
Rachel and Kirsty. "I might have
known. What do you mean by this?"

"Well…" Rachel said timidly, scuffing her foot along the ground. She hesitated, so it would seem as if she didn't want to tell him anything.

"I'm waiting!" he snapped in an icy voice.

"We were trying to get the Festive Spirit back for the fairies," Kirsty said after a few moments.

"Of course," Jack Frost said, still glaring. "Meddling again. How did you get here?"

"Our friend Gabriella the Snow Kingdom Fairy brought us to Fairyland," Rachel told him meekly.

"Ahh, she did, eh? And where is she now?" Jack Frost asked, leaning forwards on his throne.

Rachel and Kirsty exchanged glances. They didn't want to tell any lies about where Gabriella was, but at the same time they really wanted Jack Frost to think that she had already got the Festive Spirit.

"I...I can't see her anywhere," Kirsty said truthfully. "Perhaps she's gone back to the other fairies."

Jack Frost frowned and stroked his bony chin. "But if she came to get the Festive Spirit, why would she leave without it?" he wondered aloud. Then a thought struck him. "Unless..." He jumped off his throne with a gasp of horror. "Unless she's already got it!"

Kirsty and Rachel watched as Jack Frost rushed to a pattern carved into the floor. It looked like some kind of puzzle made from blocks of ice. What was he doing?

Jack Frost rearranged the squares of ice so that a picture of his face appeared on the blocks. Then, once the picture was complete, he was able to open a trapdoor in the puzzle and take out a silver chest.

Kirsty held her breath. That had to be the Fairyland chest, where the Festive Spirit was kept!

Jack Frost held up the chest with a grin. "Ha!" he gloated. "Your friend failed. Because I still have the Festive Spirit right here!"

Rachel swallowed nervously, and looked at Kirsty. What should they do now? She wished they'd thought out their plan more carefully. The two goblin guards were still in the room, as well as Jack Frost. There was no way she and Kirsty would be able to escape with the chest!

Spread a Little Happiness

An idea came to Rachel just in time. "Are you *sure* that's the real chest?" she asked Jack Frost. "Someone might have put a fake one in there just to trick you."

Jack Frost looked worried. "Do you mean *you* put a fake chest in there?" he demanded.

Rachel shrugged, trying as hard as she could to hold her nerve. It was difficult with Jack Frost staring right at her! "You won't know until you look, will you?" she asked.

Jack Frost kept looking from the girls to the chest, clearly debating what to do. Eventually, it seemed he couldn't bear not knowing…and he opened the chest.

Kirsty and Rachel watched anxiously as Jack Frost lifted out a crystal decanter with some amethyst-coloured liquid inside. The decanter had a glass stopper studded with a glittering diamond, and Jack Frost pulled out the stopper and sniffed the contents.

As he sniffed, the girls saw a sparkling amethyst vapour swirl out of the decanter and waft all around Jack Frost's head. Then he replaced the stopper, and a dreamy expression came over his face. He smiled in wonder at the decanter, and put it carefully back in the chest.

Kirsty felt a wriggling sensation in her
pocket and looked down to see that
Gabriella was peeping out, doing an
excited dance. "The Festive Spirit has
put Jack Frost in a really happy
holiday mood!" the tiny fairy whispered
breathlessly.

Jack Frost in a good mood? That
didn't happen very often! Kirsty seized
the opportunity to ask him a question.
"I was wondering," she said politely,
"would it be all right if we took the
chest back to the fairies now? It would
be lovely to give everyone happy
holidays with the Festive Spirit."

Jack Frost seemed delighted by the
suggestion. "Of course! My pleasure,"
he said, closing the latch on the silver
chest and handing it to Kirsty. "There's

nothing I'd like more than to see everyone enjoying the winter holiday."

"Thank you," Kirsty said. "That's very kind. I hope you like your cake, by the way!"

"Cake?" Jack Frost marvelled. "For me? Oh, this is the best day of my life!"

"Let's go," Gabriella whispered, "before the effects of the Festive Spirit wear off!"

Rachel, Kirsty and
Gabriella left the
throne room and
made their way
out of the castle very
quickly. They didn't
want Jack Frost to change his mind!

Outside, Gabriella did a loop-the-loop
in the air with delight. "Fantastic work,
girls," she cried. "You were brilliant
in there!"

"Is there enough Festive Spirit left for the Winter Festival tomorrow?" Rachel couldn't help wondering. "It seemed as if a lot came out when Jack Frost opened the decanter."

Gabriella smiled. "Don't worry," she said. "The Festive Spirit replenishes itself overnight. There will be plenty more by the morning to ensure that tomorrow's festival is a great success." She patted the chest happily and tucked it under one arm. "Thanks again," she said. "The winter holiday has been saved, and it's all down to you. Everyone will be in a happy mood, now that I've got the Festive Spirit. I'll send you back to your world now to enjoy the rest of your holiday – and the festival too, of course!"

"We will," Rachel assured her, waving to the little fairy. "Thanks, Gabriella. Goodbye!"

"Goodbye!" Kirsty called, as Gabriella waved her wand over them again.

Everything blurred as they were whisked away by fairy magic. Seconds later, they were their normal size and back at the resort in their ski outfits...and could hear whoops of laughter coming from the nearby ski slopes.

Kirsty grinned at the sound. "It seems like the Festive Spirit is working already," she said.

"Hooray for happy holidays!" Rachel cheered.

Quest for Fire

Contents

A Winter Chill

The next day, Kirsty and Rachel spent hours on the slopes, skiing and snowboarding. Gabriella's Festive Spirit was working wonderfully – everyone was having lots of fun, laughing and smiling and really enjoying themselves.

"That was great," Rachel said happily, as they headed back to their chalet later that afternoon. "I'm looking forward to warming up in front of the fire now, though, I'm freezing!"

"Me too," Kirsty said. "I do love having a big roaring fire in the chalet every evening. It gets so cosy in there."

But when they went inside, both girls were surprised and disappointed to discover that there *was* no fire. Mr Tate was crouching in front of the hearth looking fed up.

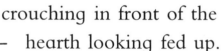

"I can't get it to light," he told the girls. "We've all had a go, but the flame won't catch."

Rachel shivered. "It's so cold in here," she said.

Mrs Walker hugged her for warmth. "Don't worry," she said. "We'll just have to head down to the village earlier than we'd planned. The Winter Festival starts soon, and there'll be a big bonfire. We can warm up in front of that."

"There are going to be fireworks later, as well," said Mrs Tate. "And a marketplace selling gifts."

"And best of all," Mr Walker said, pulling on his coat, "some stalls selling hot food and drink. What are we waiting for?"

Kirsty and Rachel went to the cloakroom area to put on their coats, hats and scarves again. As Rachel picked up her gloves, a burst of sparkles floated up from one of them…and out flew Gabriella!

"Oh girls," she said urgently. "I need your help again – and fast! I've got to find the Magic Firestone as soon as possible!"

Kirsty glanced towards the main living room of the chalet where her parents were, and dived into the little bathroom nearby, with Gabriella and Rachel following. "We mustn't let our parents see you," she whispered. "What's happened?"

"The Magic Firestone is kept in the hearth of the Grand Hall in the Fairyland palace," Gabriella explained. "It ensures that humans and fairies can light fires for warmth and cooking. But Jack Frost was so angry about being outwitted into giving back the Festive Spirit, he sent his goblins to steal the firestone and hide it in the human world.

And now the firestone is missing, there can be no fire in the human world or Fairyland. Jack Frost is determined to ruin the winter holiday fun!"

"So that's why our parents couldn't light a fire here in the chalet," Kirsty realised.

"Yes," Gabriella said. "I'm sure the goblins with the firestone are somewhere amongst the festival celebrations right here in the village."

"We're going there with our families," Rachel said. "We'll help you search for goblins – and the firestone! What does it look like?"

"It looks likes an ordinary rock, but it's surrounded by magical flames," Gabriella said. "If you see any sort of flame, the firestone is sure to be nearby."

Gabriella hid in the folds of Rachel's scarf, and the two girls slipped out of the bathroom. "Ready when you are!" Kirsty called to her parents.

The two families set off into the village. It was dark now, but strings of twinkling fairy lights had been hung from the branches of the trees, showing the way to the festival. There were crowds of adults and children, bundled up in thick winter coats and hats,

thronging around the market stalls that
lined the cobbled village street.

"Where's the bonfire?" Rachel
wondered, trying to peer through the
crowd.

"I heard it was going to be in the
market square," Mr Walker replied.
"Just along here."

They squeezed their way through the stalls, which were selling festive gingerbread, painted wooden toys, furry mittens and all sorts of other gifts. "Here's the square," Mr Tate said, as they came out at the end of the street. "Oh dear," he added, as he saw the huge unlit bonfire in the centre. "It seems as if *they're* having trouble getting their fire started, too!"

Rachel and Kirsty stood and watched as a couple of men tried to light the enormous bonfire. "I can't even get a spark, let alone a flame from these matches," they heard one of the men grumble. "What are we going to do when it's time to set off the fireworks?"

Kirsty nudged Rachel. This was all because the Magic Firestone was missing! If they couldn't find the firestone in time, the bonfire and fireworks would never be lit, and the festival's finale would be ruined!

Green Elves!

Mrs Tate gave each of the girls some money. "Do have a look round the stalls on your own, if you want," she told them. "Let's meet back here in an hour."

Rachel and Kirsty were pleased. "Now we can look for the firestone," Rachel murmured after they'd said goodbye to their parents.

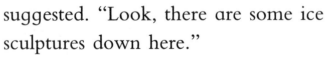

"Remember to watch out for any flame, or goblins!" Gabriella reminded them, peeking out from Rachel's fluffy scarf.

"Let's wander around this side of the square," Kirsty suggested. "Look, there are some ice sculptures down here."

The friends headed for the ice statues Kirsty had spotted. A couple of sculptors were carving shapes from huge blocks of ice with fine silver chisels. There was an ice swan, an ice polar bear with an ice fish in its mouth, and even an ice rabbit, with its ears pricked up.

"No sign of the firestone, though," Gabriella sighed, gazing around. "Let's look at the rest of the stalls around here."

The girls walked along, looking carefully for any sign of flames. After a while, they saw a stall which claimed to be run by "Santa's Elves". There were quite a few people gathered around this stall, which appeared to be selling "Toasted Bogmallows".

"Bogmallows?" Kirsty read in surprise. "What are they?" She and Rachel went closer to see. The bogmallows looked just like large green marshmallows.

Then Rachel noticed how green the "elves" running the stall were too. "Goblins!" she hissed to her friends.

"And there's the firestone!" Gabriella added in an excited whisper. She pointed a finger to where a large glowing stone, about the size of a pear, sat on the counter, surrounded by a magical flame.

Above it was fixed a metal grill, on which were scattered piles of gooey green marshmallows.

Gabriella shook her head. "I can't believe they're using such a powerful stone to warm their wretched bogmallows," she tutted. "But I'm glad we know where it is, at least."

Rachel watched as people queued up, paid, and were told to help themselves to their toasted bogmallows from the counter. "Is the firestone very hot?" she asked Gabriella in a low voice.

Gabriella shook her head. "It isn't hot to the touch," she replied. "It's heating the bogmallows with special fiery magic."

"Maybe Kirsty and I should buy a bogmallow each and try to grab it?" Rachel suggested.

"Good idea," Gabriella said.

Kirsty agreed. "Let's give it a try!"

An Ice
Idea!

Rachel and Kirsty joined the queue for
bogmallows. They pulled their hats low
over their eyes and wound their scarves
higher around their faces, hoping
the goblins wouldn't recognise them.
The goblins were very busy, though,
opening new bags of bogmallows for
toasting and counting out change,
and some were deep in conversation
at the back of the stall.

The girls handed over their money. "Help yourselves!" said a goblin wearing a white apron, putting the coins in a pot.

Kirsty took a bogmallow and stretched out her hand to grab the firestone. But just as her fingers were about to close around it, a goblin hand snatched it away.

Rachel took a bogmallow too, and the girls moved to the side of the stall.

"Rats," Kirsty muttered. "I nearly had it then!"

"We'll have to think of another plan," Rachel said, nibbling her bogmallow. It was delicious – just like a toasted marshmallow.

The two girls and Gabriella all pricked up their ears as they heard what the goblins were discussing.

"Jack Frost already has everything he needs," one of the goblins grumbled. "How are we meant to think of a good present to give him at the party?"

"You know what he's like," a second goblin complained. "He'll be really angry if we don't find a perfect gift."

The goblin in the white apron, who'd been working at the front of the stall, turned to face the chattering goblins, his hands on his hips. "If you don't start helping to sell these  bogmallows, we won't raise enough money to buy *anything*!" he snapped.

"Hmmm," Rachel said. "Maybe if we offer the goblins a present for Jack Frost, they'll agree to swap the firestone for it."

"Good idea," Kirsty said, "but what? It would have to be something amazing to make them want to swap. Something really special."

The three friends thought hard for a few moments, then an idea popped into Rachel's head. "Gabriella, would you be able to create an ice statue, like the ones we saw the sculptors working at earlier?"

"Of course," Gabriella replied, "but why?"

Rachel grinned. "I've thought of the perfect present for Jack Frost," she explained. "An ice sculpture of himself! It would be a great centrepiece for his party!"

Kirsty's face lit up. "That's brilliant," she laughed.

"We all know how vain Jack Frost is," Gabriella agreed. "He'll love it!"

Quickly, they all moved out of sight of the crowds. Gabriella waved her wand and a large block of ice appeared. With a few sprinkles of fairy dust, a statue was created in a perfect likeness of Jack Frost. The ice figure wore robes and a glittering ice crown.

"Wow," Rachel said. "That's fantastic!"

"It won't last forever, of course," Gabriella said. "Even in Jack Frost's freezing castle. But it should last as long as the party does."

"That'll be fine," Kirsty said with a smile. "Now all we have to do is convince the goblins to swap it for the firestone!"

Gift-Wrapped

Gabriella sprinkled fairy dust on the
statue to make it easy to carry, then
returned to her hiding place in Rachel's
scarf. Kirsty and Rachel lifted the frozen
sculpture and took it very carefully
back to the goblins' stall.

"We've sold out,"
the goblin in the
apron shouted to
the others. He
rattled the pot of
coins. "So, what
are we going to
spend this lot on,
then? Who's thought
of a good present for Jack Frost?"

There was an uneasy silence as all
the other goblins looked at one
another, then shuffled their feet.

"*We've* thought of a good present!"
Rachel called, as she and Kirsty carried
the statue nearer the stall. Then
Gabriella leaned out from her hiding
place and pointed her wand at the
statue. With a bright blue flash of fairy

magic, the statue rose from the girls' hands and floated to the stall.

"Aarrrgh!" the goblins all screamed in chorus, thinking it was their master, come to surprise them.

"It's a statue, carved from ice," Kirsty said, trying not to giggle at the panicking goblins. "Good, isn't it? We could do a swap – you give us the firestone and in return you get this fabulous statue as a present for Jack Frost!"

The goblins looked relieved. "It does look like him," one of them said, leaning over the counter for a better view. "But…"

"But what?" Rachel prompted.

"Well, it doesn't look much like a present, does it?" the goblin said, wrinkling his long nose.

"What do you mean?" Kirsty asked.

"What *should* a present look like?"

The goblin shrugged. "Well, you know, it should be wrapped up in paper, with a ribbon to untie, and…"

Gabriella fluttered out from Rachel's scarf. "So if we gift-wrap the statue, it'll be good enough?" she asked.

The goblins looked at one another. "Well, we haven't got anything better, have we?" one of them murmured. That seemed to make their minds up. They turned back to the girls. "Yes," the goblin with the white apron said. "It's a deal – we'll swap it for the firestone, if you wrap up the statue nicely."

"OK,"
Gabriella said.
She waved her
wand at the
statue, and
fairy dust flew
all about it.
Seconds later,
the statue was
covered in holly-
patterned paper,
with a white velvet
ribbon tied around it.

"Yay!" cheered the goblins, jumping
up and down.

"The fireworks will be starting in two
minutes!" a man with a loud-hailer
announced just then. "If we can get
them to light, that is," he added.

"Please make your way down to the market square."

Rachel held out her hand for the firestone. She had to get it back for Gabriella before the fireworks were all ruined. "Firestone, please," she said to the goblins. But before it could be passed to her, there was a blast of freezing wind…and Jack Frost himself appeared!

Rachel and Kirsty ducked behind the stall before he saw them, and Gabriella darted behind the "Toasted Bogmallows" sign. Luckily, most of the festival-goers were making their way down to the market square and had their backs to the stall, so they didn't notice the unusual arrival.

Jack Frost did not seem to be in a good mood. Kirsty held her breath as he stalked over to the goblins. She really didn't want him to spot her, Rachel or Gabriella. He would be furious if he knew they were trying to get the firestone!

"The party's about to start," Jack
Frost said, in an icy voice. "I want
to know where my present is!"

"It's here!" the goblins cried, rushing
out from behind the counter. "It's right
here. Open it!"

Jack Frost's gaze fell upon
the green parcel and his
eyes glittered at the sight.
He untied the ribbon
and pulled off the
wrapping paper.

Rachel and
Kirsty watched
anxiously as
Jack Frost
stared at the
ice sculpture
of himself. His
cold, spiky face
was without any
expression. He
seemed speechless.

Rachel huddled
closer to Kirsty, feeling

very tense. Both girls knew
what a fearsome temper Jack
Frost had. If he didn't like
the gift, there was sure to
be trouble – and then
they would never get
the firestone back!

Fireworks!

"It's… It's…" Jack Frost stuttered.

Then he smiled. "It's fantastic!" He walked all around the statue, looking at every detail. "Quite astonishing. The sculptor has captured my mesmerising star quality *perfectly*."

The goblins grinned and high-fived one another as Jack Frost struck a heroic pose just like that of the statue.

"Wonderful," he said happily. "The best present ever!"

Kirsty nudged Rachel in excitement. "He loves it!" she whispered.

Jack Frost clapped his hands. "Well done, goblins!" he said. "I'll make sure

you all have a great time at the party tonight. I'll take this back to Fairyland now. See you later!" And he vanished, in another freezing icy gale.

Rachel and Kirsty came out from their hiding place. "A deal's a deal," Rachel said to the goblins, holding out her hand again. "Now can we have the firestone, please?"

The goblins were almost jumping with joy. It was obvious Jack Frost didn't usually speak so warmly to them.

"Here it is," the goblin in the white apron said, giving Rachel the firestone. "Let's go to the party!" the other goblins cheered, and off they all went.

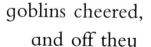

Rachel held the firestone out to Gabriella, who touched it with her wand, shrinking it so that she'd be able to take it back to Fairyland.

"Thank you once again for all your help," the beaming fairy said, kissing both the girls. "What would I do without you? Now I'd better go back to Fairyland to restore the Magic

Firestone to its rightful place in the palace hearth, so that the festival fireworks can begin!"

"Bye, Gabriella," Kirsty said. "I really enjoyed our adventures."

"Me too," Rachel said. "Goodbye!"

Gabriella waved a hand and then flew away, a bright blue spark of light against the dark night sky.

"We'd better go to meet our parents," Kirsty said as they watched the fairy disappear.

The two girls walked towards the bonfire. As they went, a great cheer rose up from the market square – and as they reached the end of the street, they saw that the bonfire had finally

been lit and bright flames were crackling all over the wood.

"Gabriella must have returned the firestone," Rachel said with a smile. "That was quick!"

"Just in time," Kirsty said happily, linking an arm through Rachel's.

"Come on, let's run, before the fireworks begin!"

The two friends raced to join their parents, and warmed their hands by the blazing bonfire. Moments later, the first fireworks went off with pops and bangs. The sky was filled with amazing colours and showers of bright sparks, and the whole crowd oohed and ahhed in delight.

"Oh, I'm so glad we could help Gabriella the Snow Kingdom Fairy," Rachel said to Kirsty as they watched a firework explode in a flash of blue and red sparks.

Kirsty nodded. "Me too," she said. "We've helped make a wonderful winter holiday for everyone!"

Now it's time for Kirsty and Rachel to help...

Ashley the Dragon Fairy

Read on for a sneak peek...

"Bye, Mum, bye, Dad!" Kirsty Tate yelled, waving as her parents' car pulled away.

Her mum, who was in the passenger seat, rolled down the window. "See you next week," she called. "And have a wonderful time, both of you!"

Kirsty grinned at her best friend, Rachel Walker. "We will!" both girls chorused. A whole week away at an outdoor adventure camp – it was going to be just perfect!

"Hi guys," came a voice from behind them. They turned to see a tall, smiling girl with long brown hair, whose red T-shirt had "Adventure Camp Counsellor" printed on in yellow letters. "You must be Kirsty and Rachel," she said. "I'm Lucy, one of the counsellors here. I'll take you to your cabin, OK?"

Kirsty and Rachel followed Lucy along a path, feeling very excited. They passed through a small wooded area where Rachel spotted a squirrel bounding up one of the pine trees, and then out to a sunny meadow with rolling hills beyond it. There were wooden cabins dotted here and there, each with colourful curtains at the window, and brightly painted front doors...

Read Ashley the Dragon Fairy to find out what adventures are in store for Kirsty and Rachel!

Meet the fairies, play games
and get sneak peeks at
the latest books!

www.rainbowmagicbooks.co.uk

There's fairy fun for everyone on
our wonderful website.
You'll find great activities, competitions, stories and
fairy profiles, and also a special newsletter.

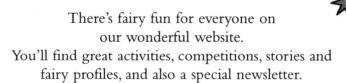

Get 30% off all Rainbow Magic books at

www.rainbowmagicbooks.co.uk

Enter the code RAINBOW at the checkout.
Offer ends 31 December 2012.

Offer valid in United Kingdom and Republic of Ireland only.

Win Rainbow Magic Goodies!

There are lots of Rainbow Magic fairies, and we want to know which one is your favourite! Send us a picture of her and tell us in thirty words why she is your favourite and why you like Rainbow Magic books. Each month we will put the entries into a draw and select one winner to receive a Rainbow Magic Sparkly T-shirt and Goody Bag!

Send your entry on a postcard to Rainbow Magic Competition, Orchard Books, 338 Euston Road, London NW1 3BH. Australian readers should email: childrens.books@hachette.com.au New Zealand readers should write to Rainbow Magic Competition, 4 Whetu Place, Mairangi Bay, Auckland NZ. Don't forget to include your name and address. Only one entry per child.

Good luck!

Christmas fun
with the fairies!

Look out for the fabulous Rainbow Magic specials.
Each one features three new adventures for
Kirsty, Rachel and a special fairy friend!

www.rainbowmagicbooks.co.uk